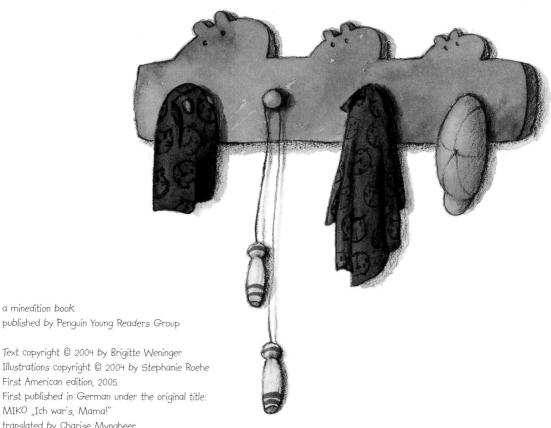

a minedition book
published by Penguin Young Readers Group

Text copyright © 2004 by Brigitte Weninger
Illustrations copyright © 2004 by Stephanie Roehe
First American edition, 2005
First published in German under the original title:
MIKO „Ich war's, Mama!"
translated by Charise Myngheer
Coproduction with Michael Neugebauer Publishing Ltd. Hong Kong.

Published simultaneously in Canada.
ISBN 0-698-40014-3
Manufactured in Hong Kong by Wide World Ltd.
Designed by Michael Neugebauer
Typesetting in Kidprint MT
Color separation by Fotoreproduzioni Grafiche, Verona, Italy.
Library of Congress Cataloging-in-Publication Data available upon request.

10 9 8 7 6 5 4 3 2 1
First Impression

Brigitte Weninger

MIKO

"It Was Me, Mom!"

Illustrated by
Stephanie Roehe

minedition

Miko knew he wasn't allowed to play ball in the house. But he and his little friend, Mimiki, wanted to know if his new rubber ball could bounce high enough to reach the ceiling.
"We have to try it!" said Miko to Mimiki. "Just once. Three...two...one...Goooooo...!"

The little ball bounced high into the air and made it
all the way to the ceiling!  When it came down,
it bounced on the floor and flew toward Mom's
most favorite vase, the yellow one with the red
polka dots.  Crash!
"Oh, no!" whispered Miko.

"Quick!" Miko said to Mimiki. "We have to pick up the pieces before
Mom gets back."
But Mimiki had his own problems. He was lying in a huge puddle of water.
"Oh, great," complained Miko as he fished Mimiki out. "Why do things
like this always happen to me?"

Miko dried Mimiki off. He stuck the flowers in the coffee pot, and then he cleaned up the mess.

Miko hid the dustpan full of broken glass under his bed.

"Dumb vase!" Miko complained. "Mom will be mad when she finds out! Maybe we won't get dessert anymore. What if we don't ever get to watch TV again? Or...Or..."

But Miko couldn't think of anything that could be worse than that. "Let's not tell her," decided Miko. "But what can we say when she asks where it is?"

They both thought some more.

"I know what we can say!" said Miko suddenly. "We can tell Mom that a robber broke in and stole it!" But just talking about a robber frightened them both.

"I don't think that will work," said Miko.

"We have to think of something else."

Then they heard the front door close.
"Oh, no! Mom's home!" said Miko.
"What are we going to do?"

Mom was putting the groceries away as the kitchen door opened slowly. Little Mimiki peeked in and said with his squeaky voice, "Mom, I have something terrible to tell you, but you have to promise that you won't get too mad at me."

"You're too small for me to get very mad at you," promised Mom.

So Mimiki told Mom about the ball, the vase, and the puddle of water. But he didn't tell her about Miko.

"That's too bad," said Mom. "Is the vase just cracked or is it completely broken?"

"I'll go get it," said Mimiki, and he disappeared.

Soon Mimiki was back with Miko and the broken pieces.

"Did you hear what happened?" asked Miko.

"Yeah," nodded Mom. "Mimiki told me everything."

"Well, he didn't tell you everything," admitted Miko. "I was there, too. Are you mad?"

"Not really," answered Mom. "I'm just sad. It was my favorite vase."

"Maybe we could glue it back together," said Miko. "Then it would be as good as new."

They were able to fit the pieces together, but it wasn't perfect.

"It can't hold water any more," said Miko disappointed. "It can't be a vase. But maybe we could use it as something else!" Suddenly, Miko jumped up and ran to his room.

When Miko came back, he was smiling. "Look what Grandma gave me!" he said.

"You can have them for your very favorite vase, and then it can be your very favorite candy dish!"

Mom smiled too and said, "That's a great idea! May I eat one now?"

"Of course!" said Miko. "They're all yours! Wait! Let me give you your very favorite one...

"...the yellow one with the red polka dots!"